Contents

LADY
PORTIA'S
REVENGE

LADY PORTIA'S REVENGE

Lady Portia Smith suddenly stopped reading her newspaper. She looked up. A tall man with white hair had gone past her window. Now he was walking quickly down the street.

There was something unusual about this old man. There was something about him that made her look up. He had walked past quickly and she hadn't seen his face clearly. Something about him had made her look up. Had she seen him somewhere before?

No, she said to herself. It's not possible. It can't be him.

Lady Portia read the newspaper every morning. She always read the newspaper from beginning to end. This was the first time she had stopped to look out of the window.

Lady Portia read the story on the front page again. The story on the front page was very exciting. It was a story about a kidnap. A young girl called Emily Stubbs had been taken from her home three days ago. Emily Stubbs' father was a very wealthy man – a millionaire.

Now the kidnappers were demanding money. They wanted £100 000 – one hundred thousand pounds! If Emily Stubbs' father didn't pay them, they were going to cut off one of Emily's ears.

Lady Portia enjoyed reading the newspaper. She lived a very quiet life in her small cottage in the village of Little Saltash. She had lived alone there for more than forty years. She had no friends and no family. Stories in the newspaper kept her happy.

After she had read the story about Emily Stubbs for the

second time, she put down the newspaper. She made herself a cup of tea and sat by the window.

Then she saw the white-haired old man again. He was carrying lots of newspapers under his arm. This time she saw his face clearly. The teacup fell out of her hand and broke into pieces on the floor.

'My God!' she said. 'It is him!'

Lady Portia had not seen this man for many years. But she had a good memory. She knew this man's face. She would always remember this man's face.

Forty years ago, Lady Portia was a beautiful young woman. She had long blonde hair and big blue eyes. She had lots of friends and she liked going to parties.

Lady Portia wanted to become an actress. She wanted to work in the theatres of New York and London. But her parents said no.

'You can't become an actress,' they told her. 'We will not allow it.'

So, when she was nineteen years old, her parents arranged her marriage. She had to marry a man called Lord Lancelot Smith. Lord Lancelot was very rich. He owned a large house in London, a house in the country, a castle in Scotland and many big cars.

'Now you don't need to work at all,' Lady Portia's parents said to her. 'Your husband will pay for everything.'

But Lady Portia wasn't happy. Lord Lancelot was forty years older than her. She didn't love him and she hated his friends.

Two years passed.

Then one night she went to a party. At the party she met a young soldier. His name was William. He was tall, strong and handsome. Lady Portia and William fell in love immediately.

The following evening William and Lady Portia met again in a restaurant. It was the start of a great romance.

Lady Portia and William met two or three times every week. They went to restaurants. They went to the theatre together. Sometimes they spent the weekend at a hotel in the country. It was the happiest time of Lady Portia's life.

But Lady Portia was a married woman and William was a cousin of the King of England. They had to be very careful. Nobody must know about them. They didn't want a scandal. But, soon, people started to talk about the two of them.

Later that year, Lady Portia's husband had to go to

America on business. Lady Portia and William decided to have a holiday together. They went to a little village at the seaside and stayed in a very quiet hotel. Nobody knew them at the hotel. They were very happy together.

Then, one morning while Lady Portia and William were walking on the beach, they saw a young man with a camera. He was taking photographs of them.

'Hey you! Stop that!' shouted William. The young man turned round and ran away.

Lady Portia was very upset. 'I'm worried, William,' she said. 'Nobody must know about us.'

'It's all right, my darling,' said William, and he held Lady Portia tightly. 'It's all right. He's a holiday-maker taking photographs.'

But William was wrong. The young man with the camera was not a holiday-maker. His name was Neville White and he was a young journalist. He had followed Lady Portia and William to the village at the seaside.

The next morning, the photographs of Lady Portia and William were on the front pages of all the newspapers.

THE SCANDAL OF THE KING'S COUSIN AND A MARRIED WOMAN! screamed one newspaper headline.

THE DISGRACE OF LADY PORTIA! shouted another.

Lady Portia's life was changed for ever. William left England and Lady Portia never saw him again. Lord Lancelot ended their marriage – he divorced her. Lady Portia's friends stopped speaking to her.

So Lady Portia bought a small cottage in the village of Little Saltash. She went there and lived alone.

Lady Portia was now an old lady. Her hair was grey and she walked slowly. She didn't often leave her little cottage.

Lady Portia always kept two photographs on her desk.

'Hey you! Stop that!' shouted William.

One was a photograph of the man she loved – William. The other was a photograph of the man she hated – Neville White, the journalist. Neville White had destroyed her happiness. She thought about him often.

She hadn't seen Neville White for forty years. She hadn't seen him since that terrible morning on the beach. And now here he was – a white-haired old man in the High Street of Little Saltash. There was no mistake. The old man was certainly Neville White.

Lady Portia put on her coat and picked up her walking-stick. Then she walked down to the village.

On the way, she met a neighbour. 'Who is the white-haired old man I saw a few minutes ago?' Lady Portia asked.

'Oh, that's Neville White,' replied the woman. 'He was a famous journalist in London. But now he has retired. He has bought a cottage here in Little Saltash.'

'Oh?' said Lady Portia.

'Yes,' said the neighbour. 'Betty, the shopkeeper, told me all about him. He goes into the shop every morning and buys all the daily newspapers.'

'All the daily newspapers?' asked Lady Portia.

'Yes, he goes in at 10 o'clock every day and buys a copy of each of them.'

'That's interesting,' said Lady Portia.

When she got home, she sat down and started to think. Suddenly she smiled. She had thought of a clever plan.

The next day, Lady Portia went into the village shop at quarter to ten. She spoke to Betty. Betty knew everything that happened in the village. She talked to everyone.

'Do you know that big old house on the hill?' Lady Portia asked her.

'Yes I do,' said Betty.

'I thought it was empty,' said Lady Portia.

'Yes, it is,' said Betty. 'Nobody lives there. It's been empty for years. Nobody ever goes there.'

'That's odd,' said Lady Portia. 'I was walking near there a few days ago and I heard a strange noise.'

'Really?' asked Betty. 'What did you hear?'

'I heard a young woman's voice,' replied Lady Portia. 'A young woman's voice – inside the house.'

'But the house is empty,' said Betty.

'I know,' said Lady Portia. 'But I'm sure I heard a young woman's voice. Isn't that strange?'

Lady Portia said good bye to Betty. She went outside and waited on the other side of the street. After a few minutes, Neville White came down the road and went into the shop. It was exactly ten o'clock.

Lady Portia crossed the road and stood outside the shop door. She listened carefully to Betty's conversation with Neville White.

'Do you know that old house on the hill, Mr White?' asked Betty.

'Yes, I've walked past there,' said Neville White.

'Well,' said Betty, 'it's been empty for years, but some people say they've heard a voice inside.'

'What sort of voice?' asked Neville White.

'A young woman's voice,' said Betty, 'a young woman crying out.'

'A young woman's voice crying out?' said Neville White. 'In that empty house?'

Neville White thought quickly. He had read about the kidnapped girl, Emily Stubbs in the newspaper. Was this Emily Stubbs? He had to find out. But no one else must know. He had to stop Betty telling anyone else.

'I'm sure there's no one in that old house,' he said. 'I walked up there yesterday. I looked round the house. But I didn't hear or see anything.'

Outside, Lady Portia smiled to herself. Her plan was succeeding. Neville White did not want Betty to tell anyone else the story about the girl's voice. But Neville White had been a journalist. Lady Portia was sure that he would try to find out more. She walked slowly back home.

———

Neville White didn't like his retired life in Little Saltash. There was nothing to do. After one week in the village, he was bored.

When he heard the shopkeeper's story, Neville White became very interested. He decided to find out more.

After lunch, he walked up the hill to the big old house. It looked quiet and empty. The curtains were drawn across the windows. The gates of the garden were locked.

Neville White climbed carefully over the wall. He walked round the garden. He listened for a few minutes, but the house was silent.

At the bottom of the garden, there was a small stone building. It didn't have any windows. It had a strong door with a big lock. It looked like a prison. Neville White pushed the door open and looked inside. But the building was empty.

There's nothing here, he said to himself and he decided to go back home.

Then he noticed something on the grass. He picked it up and looked at it. It was a lady's shoe. But it wasn't an ordinary shoe. It was a very expensive lady's shoe.

How strange, Neville White said to himself. Why is it here?

He looked at the house again and listened carefully. Suddenly, he heard something. 'Help! Help!' Was it a woman's voice?

Neville White didn't know what to do.

He thought about Emily Stubbs, the girl who had been kidnapped. He looked at the expensive lady's shoe again. Emily Stubbs was a very rich young lady. Was it Emily's shoe? Was she a prisoner in this house?

Neville White listened again, but the house was silent. He looked around, but he couldn't see anybody. He was alone. He felt frightened. The men who had kidnapped Emily Stubbs were dangerous.

'Be careful, Neville,' he said to himself. 'Don't do anything stupid. You're too old.'

He put the shoe down on the grass and hurried out of the garden.

———

Lady Portia was hiding behind a bush in the garden. She watched as Neville White walked quickly down the hill. Lady Portia walked across the garden and picked up her expensive shoe.

'What a stupid man!' she said. 'He really is a stupid old man!'

And then, for the first time in forty years, Lady Portia laughed.

'What a stupid man,' she said again. And she laughed and laughed and laughed.

———

As Neville White hurried down the hill, he felt excited. He thought about the expensive shoe and the woman's voice. He became more and more certain that Emily Stubbs was a prisoner inside the big old house.

But he wasn't going to tell anybody about this. He certainly wasn't going to tell the police yet. He was going to make this his last great news story.

He thought about the newspaper headlines –

NEVILLE WHITE SOLVES KIDNAP MYSTERY!
RETIRED JOURNALIST RESCUES MILLIONAIRESS!

Nobody else must know, he said to himself. I'm still a great journalist. I can solve this mystery by myself.

The next morning, he woke up early and went back to the big old house. There was nobody around. It was all quiet,

For the first time in forty years, Lady Portia laughed.

but he still felt very nervous. Neville decided to sit down
and wait. Time passed, but nothing happened. He didn't
see anything and he didn't hear anything unusual.

By six o'clock that evening he felt tired and hungry. But
he was still certain that Emily Stubbs was inside the house.

This is going to be my greatest story, Neville White said
to himself. I am going to find out what's happening in that
house.

He took a business card out of his pocket. His name,
address and telephone number were written on the card.
He went to the front door of the house and put the card
through the letter box. Then he turned and hurried back
down the hill.

He couldn't sleep that night. He sat in bed and thought
about Emily Stubbs and the kidnappers. Had the kidnappers

got his card? Was Emily alive or dead? What was going to happen?

———

When he went downstairs early the next morning, there was a letter for him. Who was it from? His hands shook as he opened it. It said:

We know you are watching us. We want to speak to you. Meet us at eight o'clock tonight in the little stone building at the bottom of the garden.

This is a warning – come alone, or nobody will ever see Emily again!

He read the letter again. He was really excited. 'This will be the greatest story I've ever written,' he said aloud.

At seven o'clock that evening he picked up his camera and his notebook. Then he hurried up the hill to the big, empty house. When he got there, it was nearly dark. The house was completely silent.

He walked excitedly to the little stone building at the bottom of the garden. He pushed open the door and went in.

It was cold and dark inside. In the middle of the room, he found a table and a chair. On the table there was a candle, a box of matches and an old newspaper. He lit the candle and looked at the newspaper. He was very surprised. On the front page there was a story that he had written more than forty years before. It was a story about a love affair between a cousin of the King and a woman called Lady Portia Smith.

How strange, he thought. I'd completely forgotten about this story!

He sat down on the chair and started to read.

*Lady Portia saw Neville White reading the newspaper.
She smiled to herself.*

Outside, very slowly and very quietly, Lady Portia walked towards the little stone building. She saw Neville White reading the newspaper. She smiled to herself and then quietly shut the door of the building and turned the key in the lock.

———

One month later Lady Portia returned to the little stone building. She unlocked the door and went inside. Neville White's body was in the corner of the room, but Lady Portia didn't look at him. She picked up her newspaper and left with a smile on her face.

Six weeks after that, the body of Neville White was found by a workman. But, of course, the mystery of his death was never solved.

SPECIALLY
FOR
YOU

SPECIALLY FOR YOU

'Work, work, work,' said Maria. 'Why do I work so hard?'

She stopped cleaning and looked out of the window.It was Christmas morning. Everybody in the city of San Lorenzo was asleep. The hot, dusty streets were very quiet.

'I don't want to work,' said Maria. 'It's Christmas Day!'

Maria was a chambermaid. She cleaned the rooms and made the beds in a luxury hotel. She worked every day of the year – even Christmas Day. But Maria hated her job. She hated San Lorenzo. She wanted to leave San Lorenzo and live in the USA. That was her dream.

So she saved some money every week. But she didn't earn very much money. And a plane ticket to the USA was very expensive.

Christmas Day, Maria said to herself. And what do I get? Presents? A holiday? No! Nothing! It's no good. I'll never be rich. I'll never make enough money to get away from San Lorenzo.

She turned away from the window and started work again.

She was cleaning the floor of a bedroom in the hotel, when she noticed something under the bed. It was a small suitcase. She listened carefully for a few moments. She could hear nobody. She opened the suitcase slowly and looked inside.

'My God! she said.

Inside the suitcase, she saw two silk ties, a small brown teddy bear and thousands and thousands of dollars.

Inside the suitcase, she saw two silk ties, a small brown teddy bear and thousands and thousands of dollars.

Maria didn't know what to do.

'Shall I call the police?' Maria asked herself. 'Or shall I tell the hotel manager? Or . . . or . . . shall I keep the money?'

Maria was an honest young woman. She had never stolen before. She thought very hard. She thought about her life as a chambermaid in San Lorenzo. Then she looked at the dollars again and thought about the United States.

Yes, she thought. It's Christmas Day. This is a present for me.

She picked up the suitcase. She walked quickly out of the back door of the hotel and stopped a taxi in the street.

'Take me to the airport, please,' she said to the driver.

As the taxi was leaving, Maria saw a little boy. He had big brown eyes and long red hair. His face was dirty and he didn't have any shoes. He looked very poor and unhappy.

'Stop, please,' said Maria to the driver.

The driver stopped and Maria took the teddy bear out of the suitcase.

'Hey kid!' she shouted to the little boy. 'I want you to have this.'

Maria gave the teddy bear to the little boy.

The little boy looked at the teddy bear for a moment and then he smiled at Maria. 'Thank you very, much,' he said and he held the teddy bear tightly.

'Happy Christmas, kid,' Maria shouted. 'It's specially for you.'

Her taxi left for the airport.

———

Exactly a year later, on the next Christmas Day, Maria sat in the garden of her house in southern California. Her new husband was swimming in their pool and she was drinking a glass of cold fruit juice.

How much my life has changed in a year, she thought.

Her husband, Elmer, was a rich, successful businessman. He was thirty years older than Maria. He was short and fat. He wasn't handsome and he wasn't very interesting. But Maria hadn't married him for love. She had married him for his money.

Nine months ago she had met Elmer at a hotel in Los Angeles. Maria had spent all the dollars in the suitcase. She had nothing. When Elmer asked Maria to marry him, she agreed immediately.

Although she hadn't married Elmer for love, she liked him very much. He was a good man. He was kind to her. She was beginning to fall in love with him.

As he got out of the pool, she put down her glass of fruit juice and smiled at him.

'Elmer darling,' she said to him, 'this is the best Christmas Day I have ever had.'

'And it's the best Christmas Day I've ever had, too,' Elmer replied. 'But there's one thing wrong . . .'

'What's that?' she asked.

'Well,' he said. 'I know that this sounds a little strange, but this is my first Christmas without my teddy bear.'

'Your teddy bear?' asked Maria.

'Yes, it sounds stupid, doesn't it?' he answered. 'But my mother gave me a teddy bear before she died. For nearly fifty years I took it with me everywhere. It was very important to me. And then, last Christmas Day I lost it . . . or, it was stolen . . . I don't know.'

For the first time in their life together, her husband looked really sad.

'How,' Maria asked. 'How did it happen?'

'Well, I left it in a suitcase in a hotel bedroom . . .'

'In a hotel bedroom!' said Maria. 'How terrible!'

Her face went white. 'Where were you?' she asked. 'Where did it happen?'

'It's strange,' said Elmer, 'I lost it in San Lorenzo – I was on a business trip.' Elmer paused and then continued, 'San Lorenzo – that's your home town isn't it?'

Maria didn't look at her husband.

'How terrible,' she said quietly. 'How terrible. Please don't tell me any more. It'll make me unhappy.'

———

Maria tried to forget her husband's story. But she couldn't

29

'Elmer, darling,' Maria said to him, 'this is the best
Christmas Day I have ever had.'

forget it. She often woke up in the middle of the night and thought about the money in the suitcase. Then she remembered the little brown teddy bear – her husband's little brown teddy bear. She had stolen from her husband. She couldn't forget that.

She wanted to tell her husband the truth. But she was afraid. She stayed in her bedroom and she didn't speak to Elmer for several days.

At first, Elmer was sorry for her. Then he was angry. Finally, he told her to see a doctor. But Maria didn't want to see a doctor. She knew what was wrong with her.

I know what to do, Maria said to herself. I'll go and find his little brown teddy bear. I'll bring it back to him.

One day, at the end of dinner, Maria spoke to her husband. 'Elmer,' she said. 'I'd like to go home for a few days. I'd like to go back to San Lorenzo. I want to see my family again.'

'That's a wonderful idea,' said Elmer. 'I've been worried about you. You've been so quiet. You need a holiday.'

'I can go?' asked Maria.

'Of course you can go,' said Elmer. 'San Lorenzo's a nice town. And I want to meet your family. When shall we leave?'

'But, Elmer,' said Maria, 'I want to go alone.'

Elmer looked very sad. 'Okay, Maria,' he said. 'You can go alone if you want to.'

———

Maria flew back to San Lorenzo the next day. She did not feel at all happy. In San Lorenzo, she wasn't the wife of a rich American businessman. In San Lorenzo, she was Maria the chambermaid. In San Lorenzo, she was a thief.

When she arrived in San Lorenzo, she didn't go to visit her family. She didn't visit any of her old friends. When she left her hotel, she wore a big hat and dark glasses.

Nobody must know who I am, she said to herself. If the police find me, they'll send me to prison.

But she had to find the little brown teddy bear. Every morning, she took a taxi to the poor areas of the city. She looked everywhere for the little boy.

'Have you seen a little boy with big brown eyes and long red hair?' she asked everybody. 'He's got a little brown teddy bear.'

She asked hundreds of people about the little boy. But nobody, had seen him. Then, on her third day in San Lorenzo, she asked an old lady. The old lady thought for a moment and then said, 'I've seen a little boy with big brown eyes and long red hair. And you're right, he always carries a little brown teddy bear with him.'

'So you know him!' said Maria excitedly. 'Where does he live? Please tell me.'

'I think . . .' said the old lady, 'I think he lives in one of the streets next to the old market. Do you know where I mean?'

'Yes,' said Maria. 'Yes, I do.'

'Quick,' Maria said to a taxi driver. 'Take me to the old market.'

'Are you sure you want to go there?' asked the taxi driver. 'It's dirty and dangerous.'

'Yes,' said Maria. 'Let's go.'

The taxi driver drove slowly through the streets around the old market. Lots of people stared at Maria in the taxi. They were very poor. Some of them asked Maria for money. One man threw something at the taxi.

After half an hour, Maria suddenly saw a boy with red hair.

'Stop!' she shouted to the taxi driver. She got out of the taxi, took off her dark glasses and walked towards the boy. The boy had big brown eyes and long red hair. He didn't have any shoes and he had a dirty face. He was carrying a little brown teddy bear. It was the boy she was looking for.

When he saw Maria, he smiled and ran towards her.

'Look,' he said happily. 'I've still got the teddy bear.'

'Oh, that's good,' said Maria. 'That's good because I need it now.'

'What do you mean?' asked the boy.

'I want it now please. Give it to me.'

'You can't have it,' said the boy. 'It's mine. It was

Anna opened her bag and took out a huge
handful of dollar bills.

Maria opened her bag and took out a huge
handful of dollar bills.

specially for me.' The boy held the teddy bear tightly.

At that moment, the boy's mother arrived.

'What's happening?' she asked.

'This lady wants to take my teddy bear,' the boy told her.

'That's right,' said Maria quickly, 'and I'll pay a lot of money for it.'

Maria opened her bag and took out a huge handful of dollar bills. She showed the money to the boy's mother. The woman was amazed. She had never seen so much money in her life.

'Give the bear to the woman,' she said to her son, and she took the money.

'No,' said the little boy. He started to cry. 'It's mine. She gave it to me. She can't have it.'

'Give it to her,' said his mother. She took the bear from the boy and gave it to Maria.

'I'll buy you another one,' the woman told her son. 'I promise.'

'But it was specially for me!' the boy cried. 'It's mine! It was specially for me!'

But Maria was already driving off in the taxi.

———

Maria waited for the next Christmas Day. It had been an unhappy year. Elmer had changed. He didn't speak to Maria very often.

He always worked late at his office. At weekends, he was always on the golf course.

Maria stayed at home and worried. 'Did anyone see me in San Lorenzo?' Maria asked herself. 'Does Elmer know about his teddy bear? Does he know I stole his suitcase?'

She decided to tell Elmer the whole story. 'That's the only answer,' she said to herself. 'This Christmas Day I'm going to tell him everything. I'll tell him about my life as a chambermaid. I'll tell him about the suitcase and the money. He's a good man. He'll understand. And I'll give him his little brown teddy bear. The teddy bear will be his Christmas present. I'll show him that I love him.'

On Christmas morning, as Elmer was sitting beside the pool, Maria walked over to him. She was holding the little brown teddy bear behind her back.

'Elmer,' she said. 'I want to tell you something.'

'What is it, Maria?' he asked. 'You seem very worried.'

'I've something to tell you,' Maria replied. 'But, before I tell you, I want to give you this.'

Maria gave the little brown teddy bear to her husband. Elmer looked at it for a moment, and then he smiled.

'Darling,' he said, 'you remembered the story about my teddy bear. That's nice. That's really kind of you. And I thought you didn't love me any more.'

Maria was a little surprised. Elmer was not nearly as excited as she had expected.

'Of course, it's not the same as my old teddy bear,' Elmer went on, 'but it's a beautiful present. Thank you, darling.'

'What . . .' said Maria, 'what do you mean?'

'Well,' said Elmer, 'my old teddy bear was a big black bear and it only had one eye. My mother gave it to me more than fifty years ago . . .'

Maria looked at the little brown teddy bear in her husband's hands. 'A big black bear?' she said. 'A big black bear with one eye? But . . . I thought . . . I thought . . .'

And suddenly Maria was silent.

Elmer put the little brown teddy bear on the table.

'Now,' he said, 'what do you want to tell me, darling?'

Maria thought for a moment. Then she looked at Elmer and said, 'Oh, it's nothing. Nothing. I wanted to say that this teddy bear is . . . this teddy bear is . . . specially for you. It's specially for you, darling.'

IT'S
ONLY
A TRICK

IT'S ONLY A TRICK

Professor Lewis was a scientist. The Professor's wife had died when she was a young woman. She had died of a sudden and terrible illness. From the moment of her death, the Professor's life had changed. He thought about life and death all the time. He wanted to stop illness and suffering. He wanted to find the secret of long and healthy life.

The Professor worked very hard. He was always in a hurry.

'People are dying every day,' he said. 'We must quickly find answers to our problems.'

He read hundreds of books. He travelled all over the world. He met lots of strange people and talked about lots of strange ideas.

Professor Lewis travelled a lot, but he never travelled alone. He always travelled with his daughter, Beatrice. Beatrice was ten years old. Her mother had died when she was two. Professor Lewis had looked after his daughter for eight years. She went everywhere with him. She was the most important person in his life.

The Professor was thirty years old. He was a tall, good-looking man who wore glasses. His daughter, Beatrice, was pretty, with brown curly hair. She also wore glasses.

———

Professor Lewis and Beatrice were now in India. The Professor had come to meet the oldest man in the world. The oldest man lived in a little village high in the Himalayan mountains in the north of India. People said he was a hundred and twenty-five years old. The Professor wanted to ask him many questions. What did he eat? What did he drink? Did he take exercise every day? When did he go to bed at night? Professor Lewis wanted to find out why the man had lived so long.

It was the first morning in India. Professor Lewis didn't like India. It was too hot and too noisy for him. But Beatrice loved it. She loved all the people and all the noise.

The Professor and Beatrice were going to take a train from New Delhi to the old man's village in the Himalayan mountains. When they arrived at the railway station, Beatrice jumped out of the taxi and ran towards a crowd of people.

Professor Lewis was always in a hurry.

'Come along Beatrice,' he shouted at her. 'Hurry up or we'll miss the train.'

But Beatrice took no notice. She wanted to see what was going on in the crowd.

'Oh Beatrice, what are you doing?' said the Professor, and he walked towards her. But Beatrice took no notice.

'Come back, Beatrice,' he shouted. 'Come back. We don't want to miss the train.'

But Beatrice was standing in the middle of the crowd. She was watching something very strange. A man was sitting on the ground with a basket in front of him. In the basket there was a long black snake. The man was playing a pipe. As he played, the snake came up out of the basket and moved its head from side to side. Beatrice watched carefully.

'What's the man doing, Daddy?' she asked her father. 'What's happening?'

'He's a snake charmer, darling,' said Professor Lewis. 'It's only a stupid trick. Please come along. We must catch our train.'

'I don't think it's a stupid trick,' said Beatrice. 'I think it's wonderful. I want to play a pipe like that. Daddy, please buy me the pipe . . . please.'

'No, Beatrice,' said her father. 'Now come along or we'll miss the train.'

'Buy me the pipe,' said Beatrice, 'or I won't come with you.'

'Oh Beatrice!' said her father.

Professor Lewis bought the snake charmer's pipe for his daughter. Then the two of them ran to their train.

———

The train to the little village in the mountains was very slow. As they travelled, Beatrice played her new pipe and the Professor talked.

'India is a strange country, Beatrice,' the Professor said to her. 'You'll see some wonderful things here and you'll see some terrible things. You must learn that some things are true and that some things are not true. Always remember– only science can teach us the truth. You must forget about the snake charmer. Snake charming is only a stupid trick. Promise me, you'll forget about him.'

But Beatrice wasn't listening. She was busy playing the snake charmer's pipe.

They arrived late that afternoon. They left the station and walked towards the village. The village was high in the mountains. The air was clear and they could see for miles around. Beatrice stopped and looked all around. The tops

Professor Lewis bought the snake charmer's pipe for his daughter.

of the mountains were white with snow. Below the village, there were green fields and trees.

'It's beautiful here, Daddy,' she said.

But the Professor didn't want to stop. He was in a hurry.

'Come on, Beatrice,' he said. 'It's late and it's getting cold. We must find a room for the night.'

But it wasn't easy to find a room. The village was very small. There were only a few houses and there weren't any hotels.

As they walked round the village, Beatrice looked at everything carefully. The women wore bright, colourful clothes. Some of them were coming from a river, carrying pots of water on their heads. Others were playing with their children in the street. One little boy waved and smiled at Beatrice. Dogs and goats ran through the streets. Birds sang in the trees and on the roof of one house Beatrice saw a little black monkey.

The Professor stopped a man in the street.

'Excuse me,' said the Professor. 'We're looking for somewhere to stay. Can you help us?'

'Yes,' said the man. 'You can stay with me. My name is Farouk. I own the village shop. Come along.'

The Professor and Beatrice followed Farouk to his shop in the village square. There were piles of fruit and vegetables on a table outside. Inside the shop, Beatrice could see boxes of strange spices. There was a man serving in the shop.

'This is my brother, Asif,' said Farouk. 'Are you hungry? Would you like something to eat?'

'Yes, thank you,' said the Professor. 'We've been travelling since early in the morning.' After they had eaten, the Professor said, 'We're very tired. I think we'll go to bed.'

'Excuse me,' said the Professor. 'We're looking for somewhere
to stay. Can you help us?'

'Of course,' said Farouk, 'I'll take you to your rooms.'

Farouk gave them two bedrooms at the back of the shop. They looked clean and comfortable.

'You're very kind,' said the Professor.

'Good night,' Farouk said. 'Sleep well.'

Next morning, the Professor and Beatrice had breakfast with Farouk. As they ate, the Professor talked to him.

'I've come to talk to the oldest man in the world,' the Professor said. 'Where does he live?'

'The oldest man in the world?' said Farouk. 'He lives over there.'

Farouk pointed to a house across the square. It was a small, dirty old house with a broken front window. Above the door of the house there was a sign which said: 'Home of the Oldest Man in the World'.

'We're very proud of the oldest man in the world,' Farouk went on. 'He's more than a hundred and twenty-five years old. Lots of tourists come to visit him.'

'That's wonderful,' said the Professor. 'We'll go and see him now. I must ask him some very important questions.'

'I'm very sorry,' Farouk said. 'I'm very sorry, but you can't visit him today.'

'Why not?' asked the Professor.

'Well, it's Tuesday,' said Farouk. 'He never sees anyone on Tuesdays.'

'But I must see him,' said the Professor, 'and I don't have very much time. I'm in a hurry. I want to see him today. What can I do?'

'We're very proud of the oldest man in the world,'
Farouk went on.

'I'm sorry,' said Farouk. 'But it's impossible today. Why don't you go to see him tomorrow? Today you can rest.'

But of course the Professor could not rest. He read his books, he walked around the village square and he drank lots and lots of tea.

Beatrice sat in front of Farouk shop and played her pipe. In the afternoon, Farouk came out of his shop and got down next to her.

'You play that pipe very well,' he said to her.

'Yes, I know,' said Beatrice. 'I'm very good at music.'

Farouk smiled at her. He was a handsome man with short black hair, large brown eyes and a large black moustache.

'Where did you get that pipe?' he asked her.

'My father bought it for me,' said Beatrice. 'He bought it from a strange man in New Delhi.'

'Really?' said Farouk.

'Yes,' replied Beatrice. 'The man was a snake charmer. He had a snake in a basket. When the man played the pipe the snake listened to the music and danced. I want to charm snakes like the snake charmer. But my father says it's only a stupid trick. He says it can't work because it's not scientific. What do you think, Mr Farouk?'

Farouk smiled at her again.

'I don't know,' he said. 'Your father is a very clever man, Beatrice. But, perhaps . . . perhaps he doesn't know everything in the world.'

Beatrice looked at him for a moment and then she started to play her pipe again.

———

The Professor and Beatrice got up early the next morning.

The Professor immediately looked for Farouk. He found him outside his shop. Farouk smiled when he saw the Professor.

'I'm sorry, Professor,' he said. 'I'm sorry – you're too late!'

'Too late? What do you mean?' asked the Professor.

'I'm afraid he's gone,' said Farouk. 'The oldest man in the world – he's gone for a walk.'

'When will he be back?' asked the Professor.

'Oh, I don't know,' said Farouk. 'Maybe two days.'

'Two days!' shouted the Professor. 'But he's a hundred and twenty-five years old!'

'I know,' said Farouk. 'I know. But he likes long walks. Perhaps that's the secret of his long life.'

'This is terrible news,' said the Professor. 'We have to fly home in three days' time. I must see him. This is a serious problem. Now, Beatrice . . .'

The Professor looked round for his daughter, but she wasn't there.

'Beatrice!' he shouted. 'Beatrice, where are you?'

'Shh!' said Farouk, and put a finger to his lips. The Professor listened. He could hear the sound of Beatrice's pipe. The sound was coming from the river. The Professor ran towards it.

When the Professor saw Beatrice, he stopped suddenly.

'My God, Beatrice,' he said. 'What are you doing?'

Beatrice was sitting on the ground, playing her pipe. Next to her, there was a long black snake. The snake was sleeping peacefully.

'Beatrice,' said the Professor very quietly. 'Stop playing your pipe. Now get up, slowly, and walk towards me.'

Beatrice was sitting on the ground, playing her pipe. Next to her, there was a long black snake.

'You're a stupid girl,' said the Professor, as they walked back to the village shop. 'Those snakes can kill you. They are very, very poisonous. You must never do that again. Never. Do you understand?'

Beatrice was silent.

'I told you about the snake charmer,' the Professor went on. 'I told you he was playing a trick. Now, I never want to hear that pipe again. Give it to me.'

'No,' said Beatrice. 'It's mine. I'm not going to give it to you.'

'Oh, Beatrice!' shouted the Professor.

'It's mine,' she said again. 'I want to keep it.'

'Okay, Beatrice,' said the Professor. 'You can keep it. But you must never play it again. Do you understand?'

'Oh, all right,' said Beatrice.

Beatrice was quiet for the next two days. She didn't play her pipe again. Her father sat in his room and read his books. On the morning of the third day, the Professor spoke to Farouk again.

'Farouk,' said the Professor, 'has he come back?'

'Who?' asked Farouk.

'The oldest man in the world – has he come back?' said the Professor again.

'Yes,' said Farouk. 'Yes, he has. But I'm afraid you can't see him today. He's very tired after his long walk. He's sleeping.'

'But we have to leave tomorrow,' said the Professor. 'I must see him today.'

'Sorry!' said Farouk and he smiled.

'I can't wait any longer,' said the Professor. 'I am going to talk to him right now. That's his house isn't it?'

'Yes,' said Farouk. 'Yes, it is, but you can't go in. Please, Professor! You mustn't go in!'

But Professor Lewis wasn't listening.

'Come along, Beatrice,' he said. He held his daughter's hand tightly and walked over to the house. He knocked on the door, opened it and the two of them went inside.

'I don't like it here, Daddy,' said Beatrice. 'It's cold and it's dark. I can't see anything.'

'Don't worry, darling,' said her father. 'Everything will be all right. Come along.'

They walked into the middle of the room.

'Hello,' shouted the Professor. 'Is anyone at home?'

They listened quietly for a moment, but there was no reply. Then Beatrice heard a noise.

'What was that Daddy?' she asked.

'I don't know,' said her father. 'I'll light a match.'

Professor Lewis lit a match and they looked slowly around the room. Then the Professor looked down at the floor.

'Oh, my God!' he said, and he dropped the match.

The room was full of long black snakes.

'Beatrice, darling,' said the Professor.

'Yes, Daddy,' said Beatrice.

'Have you got your pipe with you?'

'Yes, I have, Daddy,' replied Beatrice.

'Will you play it for me?' he asked her.

'But, Daddy, you said it's only . . .'

'Yes, darling, I know. But please . . . please . . .'

So, Beatrice started to play the snake charmer's pipe . . .

POINTS
FOR
UNDERSTANDING

Points for Understanding

1 Why did Lady Portia stop reading her newspaper?
2 What were the kidnappers going to do if Emily Stubbs' father didn't give them £100 000?
3 What was the white-haired old man carrying?
4 What did Lady Portia want to do when she was young?
5 Who arranged Lady Portia's marriage?
6 Who did she marry?
7 Why was Lady Portia unhappy?
8 Why did Lady Portia and William have to be very careful?
9 What did Lady Portia and William do when Lady Portia's husband went to America on business?
10 How did Neville White change Lady Portia's life for ever?
11 Who was the white-haired old man in the High Street of Little Saltash?
12 Who went into the village shop every morning at ten o'clock?
13 What did Lady Portia tell Betty, the shopkeeper?
14 What did Betty tell Neville White?
15 Why did Neville White tell Betty not to tell anyone else?
16 What did Neville White find on the grass near the big old house?
17 What did Neville White hear?
18 Who did Neville White think was a prisoner in the big old house?
19 Who was watching Neville White?
20 Neville White found a letter waiting for him. What was in the letter?
21 What did Neville White find on the table in the little stone building?
22 The title of this story is *Lady Portia's Revenge*. Explain how Lady Portia got her revenge.

SPECIALLY FOR YOU

1 What day of the year was it?
2 What was Maria's job?
3 What was Maria's dream?
4 Maria found a lot of money and a teddy bear in a suitcase. What did she decide to do with the money?
5 Maria gave the teddy bear to a small boy.
   (a)   Describe the small boy.
   (b)   Describe the teddy bear.
   (c)   What did Maria say to the small boy?
6 How much my life has changed in a year, she thought.
   (a)   Where was Maria sitting?
   (b)   Describe Maria's husband, Elmer.
   (c)   Why had Maria married him?
7 Where had Elmer lost his teddy bear?
8 Why was Maria not able to forget her husband's story?
9 Why did Elmer want to go with Maria to San Lorenzo? Why did Maria not want him to go with her?
10 Why did Maria wear a big hat and dark glasses when she was in San Lorenzo?
11 Who was Maria looking for?
12 Why did the taxi driver not want to take Maria to the old market?
13 Why did the boy not want to give the teddy bear to Maria?
14 What did Maria decide to do on Christmas Day?
15 Describe the teddy bear which Elmer's mother had given to him.

IT'S ONLY A TRICK

1 Why did Professor Lewis want to discover the secret of long life?
2 Why was the Professor always in a hurry?
3 How old was Beatrice?
4 The Professor had come to meet an old man.
   (a)   How old was the old man?
   (b)   What kind of questions did the Professor want to ask the old man?
   (c)   What did the Professor want to find out?

5 Why didn't the Professor like India? Did Beatrice like India?
6 What was the snake charmer doing?
7 What did Professor Lewis think of the snake charmer?
8 How did Beatrice make her father buy her the snake charmer's pipe?
9 What did Professor Lewis ask Beatrice to promise her? Did she agree?
10 Beatrice looked at everything carefully. What did she see:
   (a) In the village?
   (b) In Farouk's shop?
11 Describe the house where the oldest man in the world lived.
12 Why was the Professor not able to see the oldest man in the world on Tuesdays?
13 'What do you think, Mr Farouk?' Beatrice asked.
   (a) What was Beatrice asking about?
   (b) What was Farouk's reply?
14 Why was Professor Lewis not able to visit the oldest man in the world on the next day?
15 Why did Professor Lewis order his daughter to stop playing her pipe?
16 Why was the Professor not able to see the oldest man in the world on the third day?
17 What did the Professor see in the room when he lit a match?
18 What did Professor Lewis ask his daughter to do? Why did she not agree immediately?

Have you enjoyed this book of short stories? There are other short stories in the Guided Readers Series.

There are many different books of short stories – ghost stories, detective stories, science fiction stories, adventure stories, horror stories. Here are some titles:

The Goalkeeper's Revenge and Other Stories *by Bill Naughton*
The Verger and Other Stories *by W. Somerset Maugham*
Tales of Horror *by Bram Stoker*
The Escape and Other Stories *by W. Somerset Maugham*
Tales of Ten Worlds *by Arthur C. Clarke*
Silver Blaze and Other Stories *by Sir Arthur Conan Doyle*
Room 13 and Other Ghost Stories *by M. R. James*

Road to Nowhere *by John Milne*
The Black Cat *by John Milne*
Don't Tell Me What To Do *by Michael Hardcastle*
The Runaways *by Victor Canning*
The Red Pony *by John Steinbeck*
The Goalkeeper's Revenge and Other Stories *by Bill Naughton*
The Stranger *by Norman Whitney*
The Promise *by R. L. Scott-Buccleuch*
The Man With No Name *by Evelyn Davies and Peter Town*
The Cleverest Person in the World *by Norman Whitney*
Claws *by John Landon*
Z for Zachariah *by Robert C. O'Brien*
Tales of Horror *by Bram Stoker*
Frankenstein *by Mary Shelley*
Silver Blaze and Other Stories *by Sir Arthur Conan Doyle*
Tales of Ten Worlds *by Arthur C. Clarke*
The Boy Who Was Afraid *by Armstrong Sperry*
Room 13 and Other Ghost Stories *by M. R. James*
The Narrow Path *by Francis Selormey*
The Woman in Black *by Susan Hill*

For further information on the full selection of
Readers at all five levels in the series, please refer
to the Heinemann ELT Readers catalogue.

Macmillan Heinemann English Language Teaching, Oxford

A division of Macmillan Publishers Limited

Companies and representatives throughout the world

ISBN 0 435 27210 1

Heinemann is a registered trade mark of Reed Educational & Professional Publishing Ltd

A version of 'Specially for You' first
appeared under the title 'Happy Christmas, Kid'
in the *ELF Gazette* in December 1989.

Illustrated by Fiona McVicar
Typography by Adrian Hodgkins
Cover by Catherine Denvir and Threefold Design
Typeset in 11/14.5 pt Goudy
by Joshua Associates Ltd, Oxford
Printed and bound in Spain by Mateu Cromo

99 00 01 02 10 9 8 7 6 5